PENGUIN BOOKS

MARCEL PROUST

George D. Painter, the biographer and incunabulist, was awarded the O.B.E. in 1974. He was Assistant Keeper in charge of fifteenth-century printed books at the British Museum from 1954 to 1974. Among his other publications are *André Gide, A Critical Biography*, *Chateaubriand, A Biography*, *volume 1*, (James Tait Black Memorial Prize) and two translations, *Marcel Proust, Letters to His Mother* and *The Chelsea Way* by André Maurois. He received the Duff Cooper Memorial Prize for his biography of Proust.

George D. Painter

MARCEL PROUST

A BIOGRAPHY

Penguin Books

Penguin Books Ltd, Harmondsworth, Middlesex, England
Penguin Books, 625 Madison Avenue, New York, New York 10022, U.S.A.
Penguin Books Australia Ltd, Ringwood, Victoria, Australia
Penguin Books Canada Ltd, 2801 John Street, Markham, Ontario, Canada L3R 1B4
Penguin Books (N.Z.) Ltd, 182–190 Wairau Road, Auckland 10, New Zealand

Volume One first published by Chatto & Windus 1959
Published in Peregrine Books 1977

Volume Two first published by Chatto & Windus 1965
Published in Peregrine Books 1977

Published in one volume in Penguin Books 1983
Reprinted 1983

Acknowledgements

The author and publishers wish to thank the authors, copyright-owners, and publishers of the works used or quoted in both volumes of the present work. As stated in the Preface to Volume One, only published sources have been used; and these are fully listed and cited in the Bibliography and References to Sources.

Made and printed in Great Britain by
Richard Clay (The Chaucer Press) Ltd, Bungay, Suffolk
Set in Mono Ehrhardt

Contents

VOLUME ONE

VOLUME TWO

VOLUME ONE

Le tombeau d'Albertine est près de mon berceau

MARCELINE DESBORDES-VALMORE

For
HENRY REED

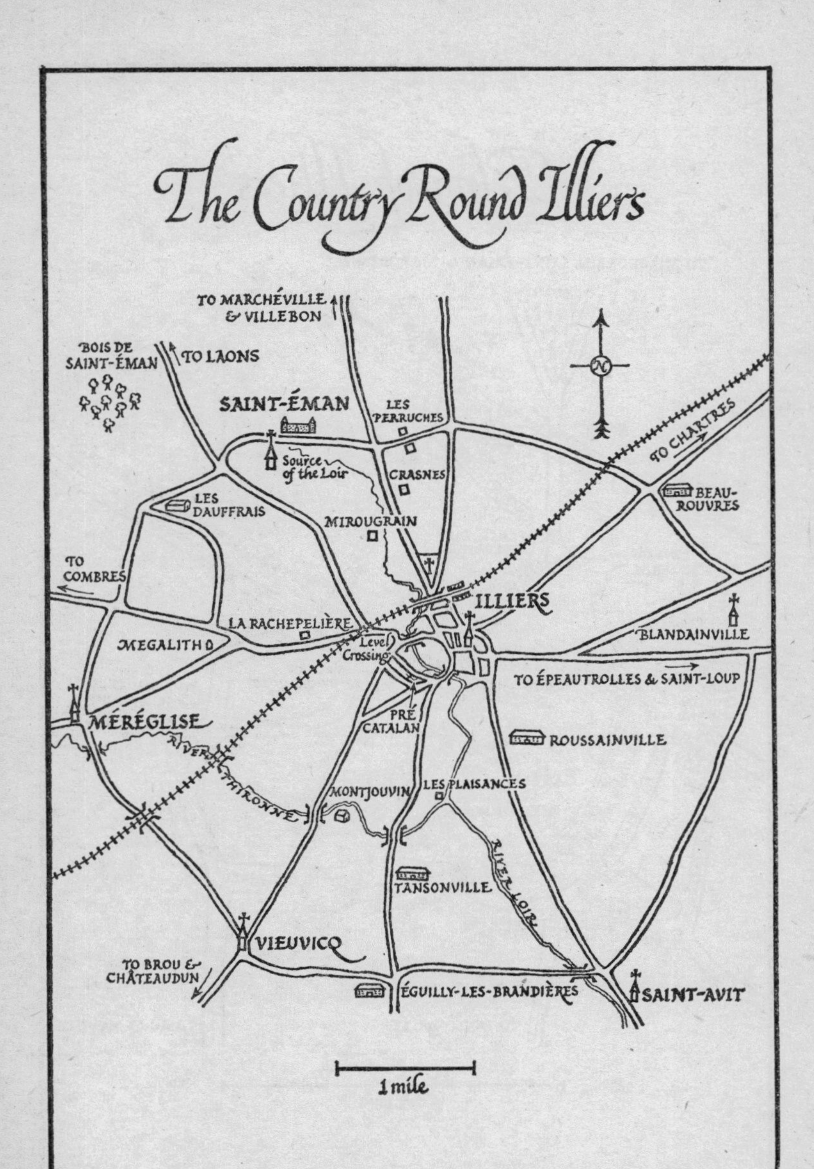
The Country Round Illiers
TO MARCHÉVILLE & VILLEBON
BOIS DE SAINT-ÉMAN
TO LAONS
SAINT-ÉMAN
LES PERRUCHES
Source of the Loir
CRASNES
TO CHARTRES
BEAU-ROUVRES
LES DAUFFRAIS
MIROUGRAIN
TO COMBRES
ILLIERS
LA RACHEPELIÈRE
Level Crossing
BLANDAINVILLE
MEGALITH
TO ÉPEAUTROLLES & SAINT-LOUP
MÉRÉGLISE
PRÉ CATALAN
ROUSSAINVILLE
RIVER THIRONNE
MONTJOUVIN
LES PLAISANCES
RIVER LOIR
TANSONVILLE
VIEUVICQ
TO BROU & CHÂTEAUDUN
ÉGUILLY-LES-BRANDIÈRES
SAINT-AVIT
1 mile

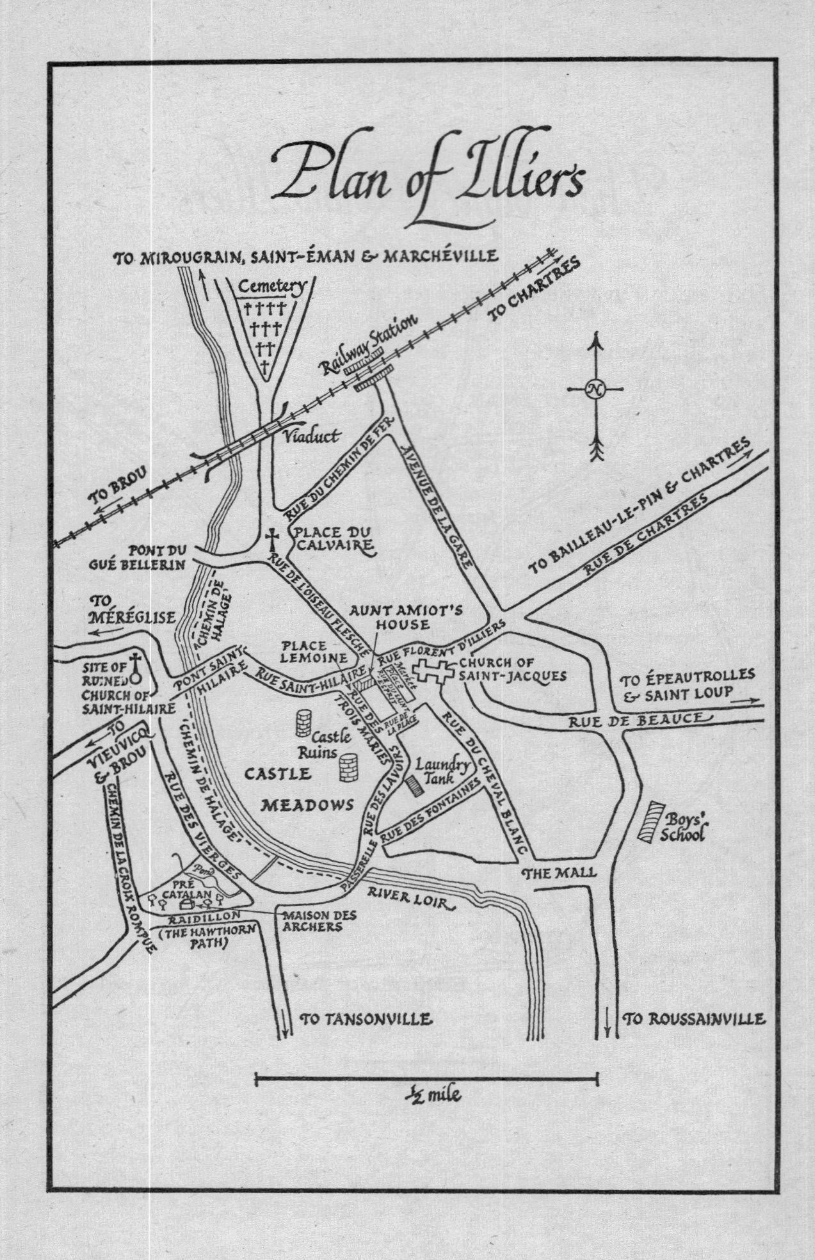
Plan of Illiers
TO MIROUGRAIN, SAINT-ÉMAN & MARCHÉVILLE
Cemetery
TO CHARTRES
Railway Station
N
Viaduct
TO BROU
RUE DU CHEMIN DE FER
AVENUE DE LA GARE
TO BAILLEAU-LE-PIN & CHARTRES
RUE DE CHARTRES
PLACE DU CALVAIRE
PONT DU GUÉ BELLERIN
RUE DE L'OISEAU FLESCHÉ
CHEMIN DE HALAGE
TO MÉRÉGLISE
AUNT AMIOT'S HOUSE
PLACE LEMOINE
RUE FLORENT D'ILLIERS
CHURCH OF SAINT-JACQUES
SITE OF RUINED CHURCH OF SAINT-HILAIRE
PONT SAINT-HILAIRE
RUE SAINT-HILAIRE
Market Place
RUE DU SAINT-ESPRIT
RUE DES TROIS MARIES
RUE DE LA PLACE
TO ÉPEAUTROLLES & SAINT LOUP
RUE DE BEAUCE
TO VIEUVICQ & BROU
Castle Ruins
CASTLE MEADOWS
RUE DES LAVOIRS
Laundry Tank
RUE DU CHEVAL BLANC
RUE DES FONTAINES
CHEMIN DE LA CROIX ROMPUE
RUE DES VIERGES
'CHEMIN DE HALAGE'
Boys' School
PASSERELLE
Pond
PRÉ CATALAN
THE MALL
RIVER LOIR
RAIDILLON (THE HAWTHORN PATH)
MAISON DES ARCHERS
TO TANSONVILLE
TO ROUSSAINVILLE
½ mile

Preface

BELIEVING that the published sources are now adequate in quantity and quality, but that the subject has never yet been treated with anything approaching scholarly method, I have endeavoured to write a definitive biography of Proust: a complete, exact and detailed narrative of his life, that is, based on every known or discoverable primary source, and on primary sources only. The mass of material is vast, complex and scattered. I have tried to winnow it, to extract all that is relevant, to place it in its organic and significant order, to preserve the main thread of the story through necessary digressions, and to serve the needs of both the general reader and the Proustian scholar. There seems to be no good reason why an interesting subject should be made boring in the name of scholarship, or why the most scrupulous accuracy should not be achievable without draining the life-blood from a living theme. Fortunately the quality of life was already abundant in the sources. I have invented nothing whatever; and even when I give the words of a conversation, or describe the state of the weather or a facial expression at a particular moment, I do so from evidence that seems reliable. I think I may claim that something like nine-tenths of the narrative here given is new to Proustian biography, or conversely that previous biographers have used only about one-tenth of the discoverable sources.

This is not intended as a controversial work: my purpose is to discover facts and elicit their meaning, and the larger part of this book is devoted to the plain narrative of Proust's life. But I must explain that my uncustomary approach to *A la Recherche du Temps Perdu*, my belief that Proust's novel cannot be fully understood without a knowledge of his life, is necessitated by the facts, and is not due to mere ignorance of the accepted clichés. It has become one of the dogmas of Proustian criticism that his novel can and must be treated as a closed system, containing in itself all the elements necessary for its understanding. To take two examples from many dozens, Monsieur X is praised for having 'emptied his mind' – did he have to empty it of so very much? – 'of all Proustian matter extraneous to the novel which he has set himself to examine'; 'I do not propose,' says Professor Y, 'in this study, which is an attempt to interpret Proust's great novel, to discuss the external facts of his life.' But they like to have it both ways. They use, and so does Professor Z, unproven biographical axioms for critical purposes: they argue (again to take one instance of many) from the supposed total homosexuality of the author, that the women loved by the Narrator are disguises of men loved by Proust, that they must therefore be psychologically unconvincing, and that Proust has falsified the whole drama of human love. I have not tried to deny Proust's homosexuality – on the contrary, I shall give the first full account of it based on evidence. But readers who have felt all along that Proust's picture of heterosexual love is valid and founded on personal experience will be glad to find their instinct justified. Here, then, is one among very many unrealized biographical facts about Proust the critical bearing of which is fundamental and indispensable. In general, however, there is no aspect of Proust or his work – his style, philosophy, character, morality, his attitude to music, painting, Ruskin, snobism and so on – which can be studied without an accurate and detailed knowledge of his life, or which has so far escaped distortion for lack of such knowledge.

This first volume is the place for analysis of the autobiographical material used by Proust in his novel: a discussion of his methods of synthesis will appear in the second volume, when the period at which he wrote it is reached. But it may be appropriate here to remark in advance on some of the further ways in which Proust's biography is significant for our understanding of *A la Recherche*. I hope those who judge this aspect of my work will consider whether the facts are true, rather than whether the critical approach demanded by the facts happens to be fashionable at the present moment.

I shall show that it is possible to identify and reconstruct from ample evidence the sources in Proust's real life for all major, and many minor characters, events and places in his novel. By discovering which aspects of his originals he chose or rejected, how he combined many models into each new figure, and most of all how he altered material reality to make it conform more closely to symbolic reality, we can observe the workings of his imagination at the very moment of creation. The 'closed system' Proustians have been egoistically contented to know of Proust's novel only what it means to themselves. It is surely relevant to learn what the novel meant to the author, to understand the special significance which, because they were part of his life and being, every character and episode had for Proust and still retains in its substance. What do they know of *A la Recherche* who only *A la Recherche* know?

A still more important consequence follows from the study of Proust's novel in the light of his biography. *A la Recherche* turns out to be not only based entirely on his own experiences: it is intended to be the symbolic story of his life, and occupies a place unique among great novels in that it is not, properly speaking, a fiction, but a creative autobiography. Proust believed, justifiably, that his life had the shape and meaning of a great work of art: it was his task to select, telescope and transmute the facts so that their universal significance should be revealed; and this revelation of the relationship between his own life and his unborn novel is one of the chief meanings of Time Regained. But though he invented nothing, he altered everything. His places and people are composite in space and time, constructed from various sources and from widely separate periods of his life. His purpose in so doing was not to falsify reality, but, on the contrary, to induce it to reveal the truths it so successfully hides in this world. Behind the diversity of the originals is an underlying unity, the quality which, he felt, they had in common, the Platonic ideal of which they were the obscure earthly symbols. He fused each group of particular cases into a complex, universal whole, and so disengaged the truth about the poetry of places, or love and jealousy, or the nature of duchesses, and, most of all, the meaning of the mystery of his own life. In my belief the facts demonstrated in the present biography compel us to take an entirely new view of Proust's novel. 'A man's life of any worth is a continual allegory,' said Keats: *A la Recherche* is the allegory of Proust's life, a work not of fiction but of imagination interpreting reality.

It would be absurd to suppose that Proust's greatness is in any degree lessened by his reliance on reality. His work is an illustration of Wordsworth's distinction between Fancy and Imagination – between the art which invents what has never existed and the art which discovers the inner meanings of what exists. We may or may not feel that Imagination is superior to Fancy; but we cannot possibly maintain that it is inferior. Proust was perhaps deficient in or indifferent to Fancy; but he was among the greatest masters of Imagination. It would be equally absurd to pretend that *A la Recherche* is a mere *roman à clef* – a novel, that is, which is a literal narrative of real events in which only the names are changed. As Proust himself explained to a friend, 'there are no keys to the people in my novel; or rather, there are eight or ten keys to each character.'

I do not apologize for the abundance of detail in this biography, not only because it is the function of a definitive biography to be complete, but because it was from the mass of such detail that Proust's novel was created. Dates of day, month and year (chronology, too, has to be regained) are given for every datable incident. I have tried to bring his friends and acquaintances to life as they were when he knew them, by describing their appearance, characters and subsequent careers, and by telling the social anecdotes which he revelled in and used in his novel. Sometimes it has been possible to discuss the synthesis of a Proustian character in one place, but usually the ingredients can only be mentioned as they occur in the chronological course of his life: collective references will be found, however, in the Index. Here, too, I have aimed at completeness: if Bergotte or Saint-Loup, for instance, have half a dozen or more originals, each contributing something of his own, I hope the reader would not wish me to conceal it. Often even the sources of the proper names are important, because they had some special significance in Proust's life, as indeed they have in his novel, of which two major sections are called Names of Places and Names of People. My inquiries into the sexual inversion, or Jewish, plebeian or noble birth of persons whom Proust knew, are necessitated by the nature of the case, and do not correspond to any prejudices or predilections on my own part.

It has been necessary to interrupt the main narrative with four long digressions: on the topography of Illiers, on Proust's hosts, hostesses and acquaintances in society, on the Dreyfus Affair, and on Proust's study of Ruskin; but these are subjects of fundamental importance in his life and novel, they could be treated in no other way, and I believe the digressions will be found not uninteresting in themselves. Sometimes the evidence on essential matters is unusually complex and intractable: my discussions of the order of composition and relationship to Proust's life of the stories in *Les Plaisirs et les Jours* and *Jean Santeuil*, and of a few points elsewhere, could not be made easy reading. But these passages are only a few pages of the whole, I have done my best to make them lucid and concise, and I can only ask the reader to take the occasional rough with the smooth.

To avoid needless repetition – and also, I confess, to avoid laying all my cards on the table before the game is finished – I have post-